THE WOLF
Next Door

BY: DARLENE KUNCYTES

THE WOLF NEXT DOOR

BY: DARLENE KUNCYTES

Copyright © at Darlene Kuncytes, 2019
All rights reserved. Printed in the United States.
Front Cover art from: Linda Boulanger, Tell Tale Book Covers.

First Edition: June, 2019
BISAC: Fiction / Paranormal / Romance / General

10 9 8 7 6 5 4 3 2 1

WORKS BY DARLENE KUNCYTES

THE SUPERNATURAL DESIRE SERIES
A Vampire's Saving Embrace: *Book One*
A Wolf's Savage Embrace: *Book Two*
Marcus' Mortal Embrace: *Book Three*

THE ANTHOLOGY NOVELLA SERIES
A Witch's Hearts Desire: *Book One*
Summer Sin: *Book Two*
Wolf Bane: *Book Three*
Magical Holiday Love: *Book Four*

STAND ALONE TITLES:
I'll Be Seeing You

Promised to a Dragon
Originally published in the **Stoking the Flames** *Anthology*

Wynter's Kiss
Originally published in the **Sinfully Delicious** *Anthology*

The Mermaid's Kiss
Originally published in the **Between the Tides** *Anthology*

The Wolf Next Door
Originally published in **The Fountain** *Anthology*

COMING SOON
Harper's Heavenly Embrace
Book Four of the Supernatural Desire Series

DEDICATION

THIS BOOK IS dedicated to my AMAZING READERS!

Your unshakable love and support, not to mention, enormous hearts inspire and astound me each and every single day. I cannot even begin to express how blessed and thankful I am to have such incredible souls standing beside me as I take this wonderful, crazy journey.

As an author, nothing means more to us than having you love the stories we tell. To lose yourselves in the places and people we create with such love is what we live for.

Thank you all so much, for allowing me to live my dreams, and I hope that along the way, I have given you characters to laugh with, to fall in love with, but mostly to make your days a little brighter and your nights a little hotter!

Here's to many, many more!

TABLE OF CONTENTS

ACKNOWLEDGMENTS

I WOULD LIKE to say a special thank you to some absolutely fabulous ladies who are truly my family. They may not be by blood, but they sure as hell are by love.

Andi and Marj. You two wonderful spirits are always there when I need you most. NO matter what, you are a shoulder to cry on. An ear to listen to as I rant...but most importantly a friend and a sister. So, thank you girls. You know I love you to the moon and back!

To the incredibly talented Linda, thank you for making my covers come alive. You always know just what I envision and I am so blessed to have you in my life!

To Grace, thank you for your selflessness and pure heart. You are an amazing lady who I am so lucky to call friend.

To my family. You guys mean the world to me and keep me going. Thank you for that!!

Love and never-ending kisses!

THE WOLF

Next Door

CHAPTER ONE

THE SUN GLISTENED and bobbed off of the rippling water dancing in the fountain, sending up shimmering flecks of light across the face of the dragon statue standing guard so regally at its center, giving the exquisitely carved beast an almost animated feel to it. Almost as if its stone-grey eyes were watching the figure standing before it intently.

Waiting.

Ember Sloane looked glanced around the silent courtyard to be certain she was alone before slipping the hood of her sweatshirt away from her face and taking a deep breath, wondering for what had to be the millionth time today if this was all just useless folly on her part.

Just what in the holy hell was she doing here anyway? She really was an idiot!

She had no idea why she had been drawn to the tiny magic shop on the outskirts of town the night before when she had been hit with the overwhelming desire to leave the solitude of her apartment.

She had gotten the need to shake off the claustrophobia that had suddenly and brutally overtaken her, and get some air. Something that seemed to be happening to her more and more often over the past few weeks.

It was almost as if she was being pulled by a strange, unseen force. A pressing, nagging sense of *urgency*.

She found herself making her way through the heavy wooden door of the store, almost as if in a dream, the tinkling of the tiny silver bells above her head sounding like music as they announced her arrival and drew the attention of the shopkeeper behind the counter.

The woman had turned as Ember entered, gracing her with a smile that seemed almost *relieved,* and Ember's pulse had quickened, thrumming in her throat like a hummingbird.

The shopkeeper was stunningly beautiful. Her dark chocolate eyes sparkled with a mischief that was surely ingrained and completely endearing. Thick black hair framed her face with perfect curls that were unruly, yet absolutely striking, and Ember couldn't help but feel somewhat intimidated just by the woman's confidence.

It was like a living, pulsating thing. Strong. Self-assured. *Bad-ass.*

"Welcome," she had called, motioning for Ember to come closer, and Ember hadn't been able to refuse.

"Don't be afraid," she had laughed. The sound light and melodic. "I promise, I won't bite."

Ember had tried to swallow and rid herself of the very large lump that had stationed itself firmly in her throat to no avail, and took a tentative step forward, the incredible smell of sage and cinnamon wafting on the air in a glorious hodgepodge of sensory overload.

"I'm Neoma," she chuckled softly. "I've been expecting you, *Little One*."

Ember stopped dead in her tracks as the words left the woman's mouth, her own falling open in shock.

Just what in the world did *that* mean?

"*How…*" she had stammered, at a complete loss and unable to find the words she needed.

Neoma tittered happily as she gracefully dashed around the counter, the multitude of bangles on her wrists jingling as she made her way over to where Ember stood frozen like a statue. The shopkeeper had taken Ember's now icy cold hand in both of hers and given it a reassuring squeeze.

"It's what I do," She replied with a wink, and Ember found the gesture strangely comforting. "Now, come tell me how we can make your heart content."

She had pulled Ember across the store and through a small, narrow doorway covered by a thick, midnight blue drape encrusted with tiny gems and mirrors that glittered in the lights above like millions of tiny stars.

They stepped through the entryway and into a back room, littered with tiny bottles and herbs. Neoma directed Ember to sit at the tiny table at its center, which was also covered in the same fabric as the doorway, and she settled herself across from her, dark eyes seemingly watching Ember's every movement with rapt interest.

"Tell me what troubles you, so?" She had asked quietly, her husky voice no more than a whisper on the wind.

There was a small, nagging part of Ember that wondered if this stranger didn't already know, and she fidgeted uncomfortably. She couldn't say what was going on, but she *was* certain that it was *something*. She stared back at the woman in silence, not entirely sure how she should respond exactly.

She felt almost as if she was stuck in some sort of quagmire. Muddled and disoriented.

It was a feeling that she wasn't particularly comfortable with. It was one of the main reasons she had never been a big drinker. She hated that feeling as if you weren't in charge of your faculties.

"At the moment?" She said, when she finally found her voice. "I'm wondering why in the hell I felt as if I was being drawn here, and *how* you could have known to expect me?" She mumbled in response and Neoma broke out into a fit of giggles, which only confused Ember all the more.

What in the hell was this woman's deal? Was she nuts?

"Sometimes," Neoma replied evenly, "We often don't know we are in search of something until that something tells us that we are."

"Oh, yeah. Well, now, *that* just clarifies things immensely," she had retorted with a sarcastic huff before she could stop herself, and realized that she was being a bitch. *She* had been the one who had come into the shop on her own. She was a big girl, with her own mind. But, she really had just wanted to know what in the holy hell was going on!

Neoma reached into the pocket of her skirt and pulled out a thick silver coin, setting it down on the table in front of her.

The coin was almost square in shape, but with rounded corners as if worn smooth with time. There were strange markings stamped into the silver that were beautiful. It was like nothing Ember had ever seen before. Delicate and ornate, it was lovely.

Neoma flipped the coin over in her hand, much like a magician might, to reveal the head of a Dragon gracing the other side and grinned, her eyebrow lifting slightly.

"Two blocks East, in a small garden square, there is a fountain," she whispered, her eyes locking with Ember's and she could have sworn that she could see something hopeful shining in them. "Tomorrow, at daybreak, you will go there and make your wish, then toss this coin into its waters. Your wish will be granted. But...think long and hard tonight on what it is that you *truly* want. Do not make your decision in haste."

"I'm sorry if I'm being rude, but just what in the hell are you talking about?" Ember had responded, her tone hinting at her exasperation. "There's no such thing as being granted wishes. And, even if there was, why in the world would *I* be given a wish?" she snapped, with a little more bite than she had intended, but this all had her head spinning. "This is nuts! Listen, lady, if you're looking to con money out of me, I can tell you right here and now, that you're barking up the wrong damn tree. This well is pretty much dried up."

She had begun to stand, with every intention of hauling her ass back home and away from this nonsense, when Neoma's hand on hers stopped her cold.

"You have had such a hard life," she had murmured, and Ember's heart twisted painfully in her chest. "So much loss for someone so young."

Ember's mouth dropped open for a second time on the past ten minutes. How could she have known?

Neoma gave her hand a gentle pat before grasping it and turning it over, slipping the coin into her palm.

"Never question the fates," she had informed Ember firmly, although her mouth had lifted at the corners in a gentle smile that was somehow comforting. "Just take it for the gift it is intended to be."

Ember had nodded, wondering just when she had wandered into the damn Twilight Zone. She had closed the coin in her fist and pushed back from the table. She stood, somewhat unsteadily, and took a breath, trying to clear her muddled thoughts.

As she had turned and hurriedly left the shop, she heard Neoma's voice trailing behind her...

"Remember to think long and hard as to what it is that you truly want..."

NOW, HERE SHE was, standing in the quiet courtyard like some kind of certifiable dumb-ass.

Ember watched silently; her eyes glued to the water as it almost hypnotically cascaded from the dragon's mouth sitting so proudly at the center, as if it were it were serving as some sort of sentinel, standing guard. But, standing guard against *what* she had no idea.

She watched the rippling depths as the water fell into the bowl, the sound of the droplets splashing onto to stones beneath with soft *plunks*. She loved the sound it emitted. It was a sound much like that of a distant waterfall and it was positively mesmerizing.

She felt light-headed again, and quickly shook herself.

She had been up half the night, pacing the floor and wondering if any of this could possibly be true... or was Neoma just bat-shit crazy.

Geez, she thought with another small shake of her head...maybe *she* was the one who was crazy. If not, why else would she be standing here contemplating making a wish like she had so many times as a child. Wishes that never came true.

Well. What in the hell could it hurt?

She took a quick breath and anxiously glanced around the courtyard once more to make one hundred percent sure that she was alone before taking the coin and closing her eyes.

"I just want to find out what happened to Evan, and to be happy again," she whispered before tossing the coin into the water with a soft, distinctive *plop*.

A nervous giggle flew past her lips that she realized with a grimace sounded more like an uncomfortable cackle than any form of amusement, and her face heated with embarrassment.

Just what in the hell was she doing?

Did she actually believe any of this nonsense?

Ember cleared her throat and turned to walk away, feeling ridiculous for having even come in the first place.

"A tall, dark hottie wouldn't hurt either if you're feeling generous," she threw out over her shoulder to no one in particular with a sarcastic chuff. If you're going to make an ass out of yourself, she thought with a shrug, go big or go home!

She really had to be the biggest idiot on the planet for buying into any of this for even a minute.

Wishes!

Yeah...*right*.

And the next thing you know, monkeys will be flying out of my ass!

CHAPTER TWO

EMBER WAS PULLED roughly from a nice, deep sleep the following morning by the sound of heavy, thudding footsteps stomping up and down the hall in front of her apartment door.

She opened one eye as a low growl made its way up her throat and past her lips.

Good God! It sounded as if a herd of water buffalo were moving back and forth!

She knew that the apartment two down from hers was vacant, and figured that her jerk of a landlord must have rented it out finally, but just who in the hell was moving in...*Ringling Brothers*?

She turned over and glanced at the bedside clock, her brows immediately furrowing with fury when she saw that it was barely seven in the morning.

And, a *Sunday* morning at that!

What in the bloody *hell*?

She threw back the comforter and slid from the bed, stomping across her bedroom and through the living room as if the devil himself were at her heels. Getting angrier with each step that she took as the cool morning air left a trail of gooseflesh up and down her body.

She turned the locks and yanked open her door, glaring out into the hallway in murderous fury. "Do you have *any* idea what freaking time it is, *Jackoff*?" She snapped at the receding back casually making its way down the hall carrying a very large cardboard box.

Ember's heart jumped to her throat when the back in question stopped and turned around. Her breath caught in her throat with an audible hiss of surprise as her gaze locked with that of her new neighbor.

Deep, intense honey gold eyes caught hers from a face that was something straight out of Esquire Magazine.

Tan. Chiseled. With full, pouty lips, and hair the color of a raven's wing.

Holy mother of *crap!*

From what she could see, his muscular arms were *extremely* well defined and masculine as all get out! And his thighs...

Oh, good *Lord!* His thighs strained against the worn and faded blue of his jeans in a way that had her face heating in an instant and her blood racing through her veins like molten lava.

"Mornin," he called, much more pleasantly than she deserved, considering the way she had practically bitten the poor man's head off.

Not to mention that whole *Jackoff* thing.

"Sorry. I didn't realize anyone was moving in," she stammered stupidly, and just wanted to vanish right there through the floor.

He set the box down and took a step towards her, his massive chest straining the fabric of the white t-shirt that he wore to what looked to be the garment's limit.

Damn, but the man was lick your lips, drop your drawers, *gorgeous!*

He held out his hand as his eyes slid over her face in a way that caused her heart to flutter frantically around in her chest, and he gave her a smile that just about did her in.

"I'm sorry if I woke you," he apologized, and his strong, calloused fingers wrapped around hers and gave them a gentle, yet firm squeeze. "I'm Bader Grant. I guess I'm your new neighbor."

Ember felt an electric current run up her arm as the warmth of his hand settled itself around her. She pulled hers away quickly, suddenly feeling like a silly schoolgirl experiencing her first prepubescent crush.

"Ember." She somehow managed to choke out, doing her best not to sound as out of sorts as she felt. "Ember Sloane."

"Interesting name," he commented with a chuckle, and she found the sound incredibly warm and husky. It was smooth and sexy in a way that seemed so easy and natural.

It was a sound that was genuine.

"I could say the same of you," she countered lightly, finally getting her footing back a bit. She usually wasn't the kind to get rattled by a handsome man. She could usually hold her own in situations. No matter *how* edible they were.

"Touché'," he responded with a wink that had her tummy fluttering.

"Well," she hedged softly, wanting nothing more than to dash back into the safety of her apartment.

She knew that she had to look a mess. Bed hair, no makeup...and she was pretty damn sure that she had a nice drool mark drying on the side of her face.

She wasn't too proud to admit that sleeping with her was very much like sleeping with a St. Bernard.

"It was very nice to meet you, Mr. Grant. Welcome to the building."

"Bader," he corrected. "Or, *Bade* if you prefer. Again, I'm sorry if I woke you, I know it's early."

"It's fine," she said, backing up.

"It means *full moon*," he called as she started to close the door.

"Pardon me?"

"My name," he laughed, those intense golden eyes almost *glowing* from the light in the hallway and she found the sight of it extraordinary. "It's Arabic for Full Moon."

"Oh." And she found herself thinking...*how appropriate.*

He nodded with an amused grin as his gaze swept over her, "And yours needs no explanation at all," he observed good naturedly.

Ember smiled in spite of herself, reached up and touched her auburn hair. "No, I guess it doesn't. It was very nice meeting you, *Bader*," she replied before closing the door.

As the lock clicked into place, she swore that she heard him say: "*I look forward to seeing you around.*"

Ember leaned back against the door and sighed, fighting off the nagging urge to turn back and peer through the peephole. Just to catch one more glimpse of the man. He was just *that* easy on the eyes.

11

Instead, she made her way into the kitchen and started a pot of coffee. There was no way she was going to fall back to sleep *now*.

BADE DROPPED THE box he held onto the floor with a quiet grunt and looked around the apartment. Not at all what he was used to, but for the time being it would have to do. It wasn't like he had much of a choice in the matter.

He ran his fingers through his thick, unruly hair and walked over to the window, looking out over the city. The scattered buildings and hi-rises were a far cry from the thick, dense woods and mountains that he preferred.

Damn Neoma and her frigging favors! He silently seethed. Although, he did have his own motives for agreeing to help her, but he still wasn't expecting what would greet him.

He shook his head slowly as the image of said *"favor"* popped into his head.

Beautiful auburn hair with splashes of coppery fire mingled throughout, framing a perfect, delicate face that hosted huge eyes the color of cinnamon and surrounded by thick, dark lashes. Her body was toned and curvy in all the right places. Womanly, to the point of distraction.

Yes, Ember Sloane was an exceptionally beautiful woman.

He hated that he was going to have to be the one to implode her peaceful little world.

Bade turned and headed towards the bathroom and began to strip off his clothes, dropping them haphazardly onto the floor as he did, thinking to himself that a nice long shower was just the thing he needed before visiting the neighbor.

EMBER WAS COMFORTABLY curled up on the sofa, wrapped snugly in a thick chenille blanket, a cup of coffee in one hand and a book in the other, when there was a gentle rap on her door.

She set her stuff down on the coffee table and threw off the blanket, spewing out a string of very unladylike curses under her breath as she did.

She hadn't slept well the night before, having been plagued by strange nightmares of dense fog and cloaked figures and images of Evan calling for help, and now *this!*

It wasn't bad enough *Man-meat* had woken her up at the ass crack of dawn, but now her day of laying around like broccoli and trying to shake off this strange feeling that was nagging at her like a bad tooth, was being interrupted. Ugh!

She threw open the door with every intention of getting rid of whoever it was in record time, only to find herself once again staring into those incredible golden eyes.

Crap.

"Hi," he husked, and his voice was so low and *so* stinking sexy that her toes curled right down into the carpet at her feet. "I'm terribly sorry to bother you again, but I couldn't help but smell coffee and since I haven't had time to unpack anything yet, and since I knew you were up, I was hoping you wouldn't mind..." he trailed off and let the unspoken request hang in the air as a small smile spread across his full, plump, thoroughly *suckable* lips.

And just what in the ever-loving holy hell did she do?

She stood there and stared at the man with her mouth hanging open as if she were trying to catch flies!

Good Lord!

"Are you alright?" he asked, and she shook herself out of her lust induced stupor long enough to muster up enough brain cells to answer him.

"Oh! Sorry," she managed to choke out in mortification. "I guess I was a bit...*preoccupied.* I haven't had enough coffee myself this morning. The brain is still asleep," she rambled, tapping her temple with the tip of a finger and feeling like a damn fool. "Speaking of which...please, come in. Of course, you can have a cup."

She stepped aside and ushered him in, catching a quick whiff as he brushed past her, and *sweet baby Jesus*...the man smelled *good*.

Not just good...but fan-freaking-fabulous!

He had to have just showered, because he smelled of soap and sandalwood and water...and it was fresh and clean and *amazing*.

Not to mention even *more* distracting. As if he wasn't messing with her enough as it was!

She glanced down at the old sweats she wore and inwardly cringed, fighting off the overwhelming urge to dash into her bedroom and change into something more presentable.

She looked like a bag-lady for God's sake!

Her thick, unruly locks were still un-brushed and had been hastily piled on top of her head in what couldn't even begin to pass for even a messy bun, and she didn't have a smidgen of make-up on her pale ass face.

Could this get any more embarrassing?

Her question was answered only a moment later when he turned and caught her staring at his unbelievable backside like a starving man would ogle a fresh ham at the deli counter and she winced once again.

Ah...double *crap!*

He gave her a quick, knowing grin as he made his way over to the sofa. Sitting down with a soft chuckle, he preceded to make himself comfortable by stretching his long, *muscular* legs out in front of him as if he hadn't a care in the world.

She wasn't quite sure if she should be pissed off or not at his being so forward as to just make himself at home without her actually *inviting* him to.

Man-meat sure as hell had some brass balls on him, she thought with a slight hint of irritation. Who in the hell did he think he was?

"How do you take your coffee," she asked between teeth that were just the slightest bit clenched as she made her way towards the kitchen, silently telling herself to play nice.

If there was one thing her mother had always pounded into her head, it was to be hospitable.

Or at least *try.*

"Black."

BADE WATCHED HER with interest. The gentle sway of her hips as she made her way across the room had his body heating up as if a match had been struck. It was easy and graceful, and he thought once again that she was, indeed, a beautiful creature. Soft, feminine, yet with an edge and strength about her that he couldn't help but admire.

She came back a few moments later, a steaming mug held in her hand. She set it down in front of him before taking a seat in the chair opposite of where he had planted himself.

"I'm sorry, but I really don't have anything in the house to offer you. I haven't gone shopping," she explained with a small shrug, and the smooth, docile tone of her voice washed over him like a warm, summer breeze. It was absolutely enchanting.

"The coffee is more than enough," he replied, lifting the mug and bringing it to his lips. The heavenly liquid slid down his throat and he fought back the urge to groan. He did love a good cup of coffee.

"So, are you all moved in?" she asked softly, and he knew in an instant that she was trying her best to make conversation. For all intents and purposes, she had a stranger in her home and couldn't be at all comfortable. He knew he could be intimidating.

He nodded, taking another quick swallow. "I am. Now it's just a matter of unpacking it all."

He watched as she fidgeted as if she had something to say, and found himself focusing on how striking she truly was. Flawless.

Too bad he needed to keep things on a strictly professional level.

He found her utterly intriguing; but he sure as hell didn't relish the idea of the wrath of Neoma coming down on him if he mixed a little pleasure with his business. Just the thought sent a wave of dread rippling up his spine.

Neoma was a damned force of nature, and the woman could be positively vicious when pissed off, and although there wasn't much that *could* scare him, he had no desire whatsoever to deal with that temper of hers at this point in his life.

It would be so much safer to just do what he came to do and be done with it.

Forcing himself to get back to the matter at hand, he set down his mug and gave Ember a quick smile.

"So, do you live here alone?" he asked, trying his best to sound as if he were merely being conversational and *not* some kind of creeper. The last thing he needed was to scare her off.

"Yes," she replied easily, and he knew he had succeeded in pulling it off.

So, why then did he suddenly feel...*slimy*?

"Do you have family near-by?" He asked, trying hard to concentrate on the conversation at hand and not the full, perfect curve of her mouth, or the way her eyes suddenly sparkled with moisture in the sunlight filtering through the window at the mention of family.

He watched in fascination as she took a quick breath and proceeded to force the tears back with a conviction and strength that was damn admirable.

Very impressive.

He knew her story. For hell's sake...he had been sent here in part *because* of it!

"My parents are both dead and my brother..." she hesitated a moment, and he watched as she stiffened her spine in an almost defiant movement. "My brother disappeared a few months ago," she finished softly.

17

"I'm sorry to hear that," he responded, meaning every word.

"Yeah, well, I guess sometimes we have no other choice but to learn to deal with what life hands us." The honesty in her words couldn't be denied, and he knew that he had at least opened up a door between the two of them.

"Yes, I suppose we do." He responded gently, his gaze not wavering from hers for a moment. "But, that's still a lot of loss for one person."

"I guess it is, but I can't change things. I still hold out hope that my brother will show up at my door one day."

"If I'm not being to presumptuous," he murmured, "may I ask what happened to him?"

She seemed to study him a moment, almost as if she were sizing him up and deciding whether or not she could trust him.

"I'm sure you know the story." She replied after a very long pause. "He started hanging around a wild crowd who seemed to want to do nothing but cause trouble, and one day..." she shrugged with a sadness that was palpable, "he just stopped answering his phone and returning my calls."

That's putting it mildly, Bade thought.

"I'm sure that can't be easy. Didn't you ask for help?"

She nodded her head with what seemed an almost tired sigh, and he thought it was one of the most erotic sounds he had ever heard. He knew that she hadn't meant it to be. It just was.

"I went to the police, but they really weren't very much help. I got the whole - *He's a grown man, perhaps he doesn't want to be found, but we'll check into it for you, Sweetheart.* Now, two months later...nothing."

"I can only imagine how frustrating that must be," he offered, and she shrugged.

He watched her quietly a moment before forcing himself to get up from the couch. For some odd reason, he found that he really didn't want to leave quite yet, but knew that he had to, he couldn't force too much at one time.

Baby steps with this one.

"Well, thank you for the coffee, Ember. It certainly hit the spot, but I really should start unpacking."

He waited until she stood also before following her to the door, his eyes once again focusing on the gentle sway of her backside as she walked, and a small smile curved his mouth.

Very nice.

EMBER PULLED OPEN the door and waited for Mister *Sex-on-a-Stick* to walk past. That incredible scent of his tickled her nose and she found herself hard pressed not to sniff at the man like a damn bloodhound!

He stopped and turned back towards her, his eyes capturing hers, causing her breath to involuntarily hitch in her throat, and tried like hell not to start choking on her spit like a loser.

She really was pathetic.

"Thank you again for the coffee. I hope to see you around."

Ember nodded dumbly, thinking to herself that it had been much too long since she'd had a boyfriend. She was practically foaming at the mouth!

He gave her a quick nod before turning and walking back down the hall, his tight ass a magnet for her gaze.

She closed her door before she started drooling, and went back to the sofa, plopping down like a giant sack of potatoes. She dropped her head in her hands and groaned.

Just what in the hell was wrong with her? She was usually *much* cooler than that!

Ah, shit.

EMBER SPENT THE rest of the day doing nothing at all of any consequence whatsoever.

Every time she had opened the brand-new novel that she had planned on losing herself to, she would find herself reading the same sentence over and over again as her mind flitted back to golden eyes and thick, sexy hair. Hair that her fingers were itching to run themselves through.

Finally, having endured her brain's betrayal long enough, she went to take a shower, cursing herself all the way to the bathroom.

She needed to get out of the apartment for a while. Clear her head. Away from the distraction that had moved in down the hall.

And fast!

She didn't know what in the hell was happening to her lately, but the last few days had been anything but normal, and she needed to get her mojo back on track.

She felt at odds for some reason and everything just seemed...*off*.

She shook her head in disgust when she realized that this *restlessness,* for lack of a better word, had started when she had walked into that little shop the night before last and it didn't seem to be getting any better.

In fact, it seemed to be getting worse.

She was fidgety and unfocused, and she didn't like the feeling at all. It was almost as if there was a storm coming. Like when the air has the electrical charge in it.

And *now* she had to deal with the Adonis down the hall.

Sometimes life was just cruel.

CHAPTER THREE

EMBER GRUMBLED UNDER her breath as she struggled with her bags. She cautiously made her way down the hall, certain that *something* was about to fall from her arms and to the ground. She just prayed that is wasn't the dozen eggs she had bought.

She had gone out planning on just getting away from the apartment for a bit. She figured that perhaps taking a nice long walk through the park then grabbing a bite to eat might help to clear her head.

Instead, she had spent the day wandering around like the undead and shopping just to avoid going back home and running into *hot guy*.

She was just having a hard time with the way her body reacted when he was around. She just wanted to avoid him until she could get a firm hold on her libido and keep it in check before heading back home and making a fool out of herself by doing or saying something stupid.

She set the bags down at her feet as she dug around in her purse, searching for her keys. After a few moments of coming up empty, she groaned as the image of the damn things sitting on the small table beside the door flashed before her eyes.

Damn it.

Ember stood there a moment, gnawing at her inside of her cheek and not having the slightest idea of what to do. Should she call a locksmith? Ugh! That would cost her a small fortune on a Sunday night, and her ass of a landlord was out of the country until the end of the week.

She walked over and knocked on her neighbor across-the-hall's door, hoping the nice elderly couple could give her some suggestions, but there was no answer and she remembered they usually spent Sundays at their daughter's house.

Well...

Her only other option was to suck it up and ask tall, dark, and dreamy.

Or call the cops.

And she sure as hell didn't want to have to do *that*. This was embarrassing enough!

"Do I detect a damsel in distress?"

Ember let out a tiny little cry of surprise as she spun on her heels to find Bader standing there.

No...scratch that, she thought with a little shiver of excitement. She found him *looming* there, like some kind of sexy ass storm cloud. All dark and dangerous and *yummy*.

"I've pulled a complete doofus move and locked myself out," she muttered, hoping she didn't look half as embarrassed as she felt.

She had no idea just what in the bloody hell was wrong with her where this man was concerned. He was like damned female Viagra!

"Well, let's have a look," he whispered, taking a step closer to where she stood. His chest pressed up against her side as he leaned in and grasped the door handle, giving it a sound jiggle. "Yep. You're locked out all right," he chuckled, his breath caressing the curve of her ear and causing her body to practically *vibrate*. It was soft and sensual and had her body responding in ways better left unmentioned.

"Well, *Gee*, thanks *Captain Obvious*. I wasn't sure how a door handle worked," she retorted snidely and his laughter echoed through the hallway.

"I had to check," he explained with a slight wink. "It's a guy thing."

"Whatever," she mumbled, thinking that she might have been better off having dealt with the cops making fun of her.

"I'm sure I can get you in," he said, placing his hands on her arms and gently moving her out of the way.

She felt the heat of his fingertips on her skin even after he had taken them away, and once again she shivered as if a current of electricity had been shot up her spine.

She watched with interest as he pulled a card out of his pocket and slid it into the gap of the door. He moved it just a bit and...presto! The door to her apartment swung open.

"Oh. Well, I just feel so *much* safer now," she remarked, shaking her head in disgust.

Good Lord! Was that all it took to get into her apartment? It was a wonder she hadn't woken up dead by now!

"It's not as easy as I made it look," he laughed, reaching down and picking up the bags she had set on the floor. He took a step back so she could walk through the door and she did, painfully aware of him following behind.

The man just had an essence about him. It was a charisma that was in your face and distracting as all hell.

"You can just leave those there," she said, pointing to the small table by the door where her keys sat mocking her.

"I can take them to the kitchen for you," he offered, heading in that direction and she sighed in defeat.

Why the hell not?

Ember walked into the tiny galley kitchen and leaned against the doorframe, knowing she was going to regret her next words as sure as the sun was going to rise in the morning.

"I was going to make myself dinner. If you haven't already eaten, you're welcome to join me."

"That's about the best offer I've had all day," he replied almost instantly. "I was just about to order myself a pizza."

"Well, it won't be anything fancy, but I promise it'll be edible."

"Edible works for me."

BADE OPENED A bottle of wine as Ember got to work. He had offered to help, but she had swooshed him away with a flick of her hand saying something about too many cooks, and asked that he pick out some wine and get each of them a glass.

He was actually enjoying watching her move about the tiny kitchen, chopping and sautéing as the air filled with a wide array of the most amazing smells. He hadn't realized how hungry he was until she had removed the chicken from its package and he had caught a whiff of that distinctive scent of meat.

He cleared his throat and took a sip of his wine, a bold Sauvignon Blanc that was remarkably smooth, yet full bodied and he silently gave her props on her taste.

"Are you sure I can't help?"

She looked over at where he stood watching her and graced him with a quick smile. "You could set the table, if you don't mind."

"Not at all. Domestic bliss at its best," he chuckled and instantly felt a shot of pure adrenaline hit him right in the groin when she laughed in response.

It was light and musical and airy...and it was a sound he found himself wanting to hear again.

He knew that he was treading in dangerous waters here. He didn't need to get too close to this woman. He *needed* to do what he had been asked to do, and move the hell on.

He *didn't* need entanglements. In fact, he detested them.

No matter how bewitching they might be.

EMBER TRIED HER best not to stare at the man sitting across from her, eating the chicken she had prepared as if it were a six-course gourmet feast, and wondered how someone who looked like *that* could pack away the food like he was.

She was flattered the he *really* seemed to be enjoying her cooking, yet couldn't help but think he was merely being polite.

She sipped her wine as she stole quick glances at him. The man was male perfection personified. So, what in the world was he doing here with her, casually eating dinner as if this was all just a normal, everyday occurrence? Things like this didn't happen to her.

Ever.

The few guys she had dated in her twenty-six years had been normal, average every-day guys. Not to mention that it had been a few years since she had even dated anyone at all.

That could account for her serious case of the *lusties* whenever her new neighbor was around.

She had always been pretty much one step up from a hermit.

When Evan had been around, he had been the one with all the friends. The one who had always forced her to go out and experience the world.

Now, she stayed pretty much to herself. She didn't go out and make friends. That wasn't her style. She enjoyed her solitude.

And, she certainly didn't eat meals with hot men who looked like something that had hopped right off the pages of a Men's Health magazine!

"Have you lived here long?" he asked, and Ember jumped slightly.

"Almost a year," she answered.

"Are you originally from this area?"

"No. We grew up in Washington state, but after our parents passed, we, um, we moved around a bit for a few years. Trying to find a place we liked enough to settle down in. Too many memories back home and really no family to speak of."

She watched as he nodded, his eyes skimming over her face and landing on her lips.

A warm rush of blood hit her cheeks like a slap to the face. *Damn.*

"This is a beautiful area," he agreed softly.

The sound of a dog, or perhaps it was a coyote, howling outside drifted in through the open sliding glass door of her balcony and she watched with curiosity as he seemed to stiffen ever so slightly.

Almost as if the sound disturbed him.

Strange, she thought with a small furrowing of her brow, that a man so...*ripped* might be alarmed by the sound of an animal outside. But, that was exactly what it seemed to be. His relaxed demeanor of only a moment before seemed to slip away in an instant.

He gave her a quick, almost uncomfortable smile and stood. "Listen, I really should finish unpacking," he offered, almost hastily, taking his plate and walking over to the sink. "I hate to dine and dash on you, but it's been a busy few days, and I really need to get some last-minute things taken care of. Besides," he said, glancing up at the clock hanging on the wall. "It's getting late and I've used up enough of your hospitality for one night." He turned and caught her gaze, that devilish glint back in his eyes. "I'd hate for you to get sick of me because I've overstayed my welcome."

Ember stood and silently followed as he made his way to the door, wondering just what in the hell was happening here?

"Thank you, for dinner," he said, standing in the doorway and leaning against the frame as he looked back at her. Their gazes locked and it was as if all the air had suddenly been sucked out of the building.

Before she had a moment to think about it, he leaned forward and kissed her. Soft, warm...*amazing*.

His hand cupped her face as his mouth teased hers and she thought for sure that she had died and gone to Heaven.

It was just *that* good!

Much too soon, he leaned back. "Thank you again, for dinner, Ember," he husked before turning and walking down the hall. Leaving her to stand there wondering if she was dreaming and would wake up any moment.

BADE WALKED OVER to his balcony and slid open the door, stepping through and gazing out over the grounds and into the woods that bordered the complex. He could see a set of eyes glowing from the tree line and turned back, a muscle in his jaw twitching slightly.

"Shit," he mumbled as he left his apartment and headed downstairs and out of the back entrance of the building. He began to make his way across the field at a steady gait, heading in the direction where the eyes still glowed in the light of the moon; silently watching his every move as he approached.

EMBER WATCHED IN fascination from her window as Bader made his way across the grass, her brows furrowing in bewilderment.

Jut what in the ever-loving hell was he doing?

She watched, completely engrossed, as he jogged towards the woods before quickly disappearing into the thick trees and out of sight.

Just what in the world was *that* all about?

Ember cursed herself for being so nosey and forced herself to move away from the window. It was none of her business. Perhaps he was just some kind of a nature freak. Lord knew he was rugged enough to be the outdoor type. The man belonged on the cover of Field and Stream for God's sake!

Besides, it wasn't her place to stick her nose into his business. No matter how much she may have wanted to.

She pushed away the nagging urge to go back to the window, and instead made her way to the kitchen to start cleaning up. She needed to keep herself occupied.

It was none of her business, she reminded herself once again as she began washing the dishes.

None of her damned business!

BADE STEPPED THROUGH the line of thick pine and glared into the darkness, what little patience he possessed was teetering on the brink of extinction at the moment.

"Alright, Liam," he growled. "You really don't want to piss me off any more than I already am at the moment. I was in the middle of enjoying dinner, and I'm not exactly thrilled to have been disturbed."

Bade turned at the sound of rustling to find a tall, muscular blond stepping out from behind one of the trees. His angular face was covered by a neatly trimmed beard and his mouth was turned up in a shit-eating grin.

"Hello, *oh glorious leader*," the man laughed, and Bade clenched his jaw, trying with every fiber of his being not to just throttle the irritating ass.

He *hated* to be called that, and the lunkhead damn well knew it!

"Why are you here, Liam?" Bade ground out, his tone aptly conveying the fact that he was in no mood to go back and forth with his second-in-command at the moment.

"Well, I came about some information that I thought you might want." Liam replied, leaning back against the tree he had come from behind.

"And...let me guess," Bade snarled. "You forgot to pay your cellphone bill again?"

Liam snickered, but the grin faded from his lips only a moment later as he met his friend's impatient glare. "I figured it would be best to tell you this in person."

Bade inwardly groaned, knowing that if Liam had taken the time to come all this way, the news couldn't be good.

"Let me have it," Bade urged, although he really wasn't quite sure that he wanted to hear it.

"Devlin is aware that you've been asked to help find Neoma's fiancé," he responded. "He also knows about the sister."

"Shit!" Bade spit. "How?"

"We're not sure," Liam replied, shaking his head slightly. "But, you know how that bastard operates. If there is any way in hell that he can find someone's weakness, he sure as shit is going to find it, and use it to his advantage. Devlin gets off by playing dirty," he said, the disgust lacing his tone more than evident. "Damn, but I really hate *Bloodsuckers*."

Bade nodded his agreement as he tried like hell to control his temper. Neoma had asked for his help and he'd be damned if he was going to fail her.

Not to mention the fact that he wasn't about to let the filthy Vampire or his *family* harm a single hair on Ember's head!

"Have you gotten any closer to finding out where they're holed up?" He asked, and Liam shook his head.

"They've covered their tracks pretty damned well," Liam responded.

"He always has," Bade agreed darkly.

"Yeah, well, this bastard has been a thorn in our sides for way too long now, and I would like to finish this business with this Bastard once and for all."

"I plan on doing just that. For Neoma, as well as the pack. I'm tired of these arrogant bloodsuckers. Just let me know if you hear anything else," Bade said as he turned to head back toward the apartment. He stopped and looked back at Liam. "By *phone,* if you don't mind. You seem to forget, we're not in the mountains here. You don't need to be running around only to get your ass captured by the dog warden, or worse yet, shot by some trigger-happy jackass with a gun who might spot you."

"Whatever you say, *Boss,*" Liam laughed before shifting and taking off in the opposite direction than Bade was headed.

"Asshole." Bade huffed at the retreating wolf before stomping back towards the building.

EMBER WATCHED AS Bade made his way back out of the woods and towards the complex. She had washed *and* dried the dishes before her curiosity had gotten the better of her and she made her way back to the window like some kind of creepy peeper, and cautiously pulled back the drape.

Yes. She felt like a complete slime, but she just couldn't seem to stop herself. Her intriguing neighbor had her interest piqued and one of her biggest faults had always been her inquisitive nature. And, this was all much too good to ignore!

She watched as he walked back with a determination that only added to the masculine aura of the man, and she just about lost her shit when he glanced up at her window.

With a guilty little squeak, she preceded to jump back, trip over her own damn feet, and land smack dab on her ass with a solid thump.

Dear God.

When she had finally gathered enough resolve to pick herself up and cautiously peek back through the curtains...he was gone.

She spun around when she heard his heavy footsteps coming down the hall. They seemed to hesitate in front of her door and she held her breath, waiting for him to pound on it shouting that she was a peeping Tom...or *Tilly* if you wanted to be picky, but after just a few earth-shattering seconds, they continued down the hall and she let the air out of her lungs in a quick whoosh.

That would teach her to stalk Mr. Sex-on-a-Stick!

Ember groaned as she turned and made her way toward her bedroom, deciding that she needed to mind her business and just go to bed.

She grabbed her nightshirt and headed for the bathroom, rubbing her backside as she went.

CHAPTER FOUR

"EMBER... YOU NEED *to find me.*"

Ember looked around frantically, trying to pinpoint where the sound of her brother's voice was coming from, but couldn't see anything through the thick blanket of fog that was surrounding her.

It was disorienting, and it made the sound of Evan's words seem as if they were coming from every direction all at once.

A whisper on the wind.

She felt as if she was caught in a vacuum and the air was being sucked right from her lungs by the pressure of it all.

"Evan!" She called, her body beginning to shake as she searched in vain for any sign of her twin.

She thought she saw a figure off in the distance and tried to clear her vision enough to make it out.

Tall, broad shouldered, yet lanky and she knew in an instant at that it was him. It was him! Finally!

Ember's tears stung her eyes as they streamed down her face, and she ran towards her brother, her heart swelling to the point that if felt as if it was about to explode right there in her chest.

"Evan!" she cried again, throwing herself into his waiting arms.

Her sobs were coming in earnest now, and she tried her very best to fight them back. She had a thousand and one questions for him!

"Where have you been?" she sniffled. "I looked and looked for you!"

"Emmie," he whispered into her ear, and the urgency in his voice caused her to lean back.

She looked up into his eyes. Eyes so much like her own, and felt him slip something into her hand. She looked down and watched silently as he pressed the strange coin the woman at the shop had given her securely into her palm, exactly as she had done.

But...how?

"You need to wake up now, Emmie. There isn't much time. They're coming for you. You have to get to Bader. You have to let him know that they're coming."

Ember sat bolt upright in bed with a strangled gasp as she tried to get her bearings. Her heart was slamming erratically against her ribs, knocking what little air was left, right out of her lungs.

She dropped her head into her hands and tried to fight off the panic gripping her. She needed to figure out what in the hell had just happened.

She could feel the last tendrils of her dream slipping away from her, and fought off the shiver that slithered up her

35

spine as she tried to remember every little detail that she could.

It had seemed so real, and she knew, without a doubt, and to the very recesses of her soul, that her brother was alive and in some very bad trouble.

He needed her. He was calling out to her, and she couldn't ignore it.

She wouldn't!

Her stomach did a strange little flip as Evan's final words echoed through her brain...

You have to get to Bader. You have to let him know that they're coming.

She shook herself as she wondered just who *they* were.

BADE'S EYES SNAPPED open as the sound knocking invaded his sleep, and he jumped up on full alert. He dashed through the apartment to see just who in the hell was bothering him at three in the freaking morning. He swore to God if it was Liam again, heads were going to roll!

He threw open the door with every intention of beating the Hell out of whoever it was, only to find an absolute vision standing there, looking up at him with wide, frightened eyes that sparkled like stars with their unshed tears. Unruly auburn hair framed a perfect face as she stared up at him, her bottom lip quivering ever so slightly, and he felt a strange tug to his heart.

"Ember," he husked out, confused as to why she was standing here at his door in the dead of night, dressed only in a thin, oversized t-shirt with a giant bumblebee on the front flexing its muscles with the words "*Bee Strong*" written underneath.

The nightshirt barely hit her at the knees, and her tiny feet were bare, yet she looked like a freaking Angel sent straight from the Heavens standing there like a delicate, porcelain doll.

Shit.

"Do you know anything about my brother?" She blurted out finally, and he was completely thrown for a loop. That was about the last thing he would have expected to come out of that incredible mouth of hers.

How in the *hell* had she found out?

EMBER SWALLOWED WITH difficulty as she waited for him to answer her, trying her best to stand her ground and not waiver, even though it felt as if she had just finished running a marathon, and was pretty sure she was going to burst into tears at any moment.

She couldn't exactly be sure that she wasn't making a huge mistake by coming here. Maybe Evan had only said that to her in her dream because she had spent time with Bader earlier in the evening and he was as hot as hell, and she had been thinking about him. Maybe it was just subliminal horseshit or something.

She steadied her nerves as she reminded herself that no matter what the outcome, she needed to know either way. Either she looked like some crazy-ass, flighty loser, or this man knew something about where her brother was, and she wasn't about to ignore it. The had been much more than merely a nightmare.

As twins, she and Evan had always had a strange sort of connection, and she was willing to take the chance of looking like a fool now in order to prove to herself that their connection was real, and that he was calling out to her, asking her for help.

If she ended up looking like a horse's ass...well, then, so be it. It wouldn't be the first time and she was pretty damn certain that it wouldn't be the last.

"I need to know if you know something," she pleaded softly, urging herself to keep her tone as even as possible. She sure as hell didn't need to sound like a neurotic nut-case. "I need to know if I'm..." She was about to say *crazy*, but stopped herself. Deep down in her gut, she knew that she wasn't. "Please, just tell me the truth."

"Come in," Bade responded, stepping aside and ushering her through the door.

Ember walked into the apartment and stopped short, her eyes darting around the room in shock and a growing fear.

The apartment held no furniture of any consequence whatsoever.

There was a chair and small table, and just a few boxes scattered about, which seemed to contain nothing more than clothing.

Nothing at all adorned the walls or covered the windows. It was as if the space was still vacant.

Hadn't he said that he needed to finish unpacking?

The question that was rattling around in her head as her panic grow was: unpack *what?*

Oh, sweet tap dancing baby Jesus! Just what had she walked into?

"Ember…" he whispered, reaching out his hand, but she quickly took a step away from him, trying to make her way back towards the door in case she needed to run.

"EMBER," BADE REPEATED, trying his best to put her at ease, but he could see the panic welling up inside her like a tidal wave. "It's not what you're thinking."

"Really? Then, just what in the hell *is* it?" She snapped, and he reached out again to take her hand, but she pulled it away as if she'd been burned. "Why are you here, Bader?" She asked, her eyes still darting around the near-empty apartment before finally settling back on him, and he could see the anger in them.

"I'm here to help you find Evan," he admitted quietly, and saw her body wilt in what he *hoped* was relief.

"So, you *do* know what's happened to him," she croaked out as her face drained of all its color and she turned deathly pale. He swore that her knees were about to buckle on her as he watched her sway slightly.

Without even thinking about it, he swept her up into his arms and headed back out the door and down the hall to her apartment.

He carried her over the threshold and to the sofa, setting her down and seating himself beside her. He could feel the heat of her skin against his thigh and realized that he was trembling. He cleared his throat and gave her a small grimace, wondering where to even begin.

"This may take a while," he explained softly, feeling like the biggest shit in the world for having had to lie to her. "I hope you don't mind me bringing you back here, but I figured we might as well be comfortable."

She nodded slowly, her eyes not leaving his for a second and he saw the weight of her emotions fighting against each other. He knew that she was trying desperately to grasp everything that was happening, and wondering if she was safe with him.

"You can trust me, Ember," he promised her, and he could tell by the slight relaxing of her shoulders that there was that small part of her that knew she could. Almost as if by instinct.

Thank the Gods for small favors.

"Do you want some coffee?" She asked shakily, and he couldn't help but chuckle. Always the hostess.

"More than I want air," he quipped, and was more than a little relieved when he heard her soft, musical laughter in response. It was quiet, and abrupt...but it was there and it was the sound of Angels singing.

She stood on legs that he could see still shook slightly and headed toward the kitchen. "I'll only be a minute," she called over her shoulder as she disappeared through the archway, and he could hear her take a deep, shaky breath, and let it out slowly, and knew that she was trying her best to get her emotions under control. The offer of coffee was to help her get her thoughts in check he surmised.

She returned a few minutes later with two steaming mugs held tightly in her delicate hands and he jumped up to take his from her.

She sat back down and took a sip of her coffee. "Alright, spill *everything*," she urged over the rim of her mug.

He was silent for a long moment, trying to figure out where to begin as he gazed into those amazing eyes of hers. They seemed to capture his soul with their intelligence and depth and he could easily find himself getting lost in them. Completely and totally and *willingly*...lost.

"I know this is going to be extremely hard to take in all at once," he began, struggling to keep his train of thought on the matter at hand and not frighten her again, so he did he damndest to keep his tone as light as possible. "But I really need you to keep an open mind right now. Do you think you can do that for me?"

"Well, considering that the only reason I was pounding on your door at three in the morning like a lunatic, was because my twin brother came to me in a dream and told me that *They were coming for me* and that I needed to get to *you*...I promise to keep my mind as open as humanly possible."

Bade would have laughed at her choice of words if he hadn't honed in on the *They were coming for me* part.

Son of a bitch!

"Ember, what did he say to you in your dream? I need to know word for word," He pressed, much more harshly than he had intended, and he clenched his jaw.

Ember set her mug down, watching him a moment in silence, and he knew that she was picking up on his anger.

"Just that I needed to find him, and that they were coming for me, and to...to go to *you*."

Bade nodded, taking a deep breath and realizing that they didn't have a lot of time.

"Did you recognize anything in your dream that could possibly pinpoint where Evan was?" he asked, hoping she had been given some clue as to where her brother was being held. He knew it was far-fetched, but he was desperate. "Ember...think carefully, did anything look familiar to you, at all? No matter how insignificant you think it may be."

She seemed to consider this a moment, then finally shook her head. "No. There was this thick fog all around me, and I couldn't make anything out. Please, Bader, I need to know what's going on here. My life has gone straight off of the rails and right into crazy town ever since I made that stupid wish." Her eyes widened and she reached over and grasped his arm. "The wish!" she squeaked. "I went to this tiny little shop in town the other night, and the woman there gave me a coin. She told me to go to this fountain and to make a wish! In my dream, Evan gave me the coin that she had given me back!"

"Neoma gave you the coin," Bade replied, and she nodded her head.

"Yes! That was her name! Wait...you know her *too*?" She asked incredulously.

Bade took another gulp of air into his lungs as he steadied himself. He needed to get this over with.

She deserved to know the truth.

"We're friends," he explained. "We grew up together, and she's more of a sister to me than my own flesh and blood. She and Evan were planning to be married before he was taken." He placed his hand gently over hers where she still gripped his arm and experienced a strange sort of hum at the contact. He shook it off and gave her a small smile. "This is where the open mind part comes in to play," he continued. "Your brother has been taken by a group of vampires he had been...*associating* with."

He watched as Ember's eyes grew very large, and her mouth dropped open.

She pulled her hand from his very slowly as the blood drained from her face, and he knew that she was debating on whether or not he was a complete nut-case or not, and trying to decide if she should just call it a day and run like hell.

He could see the disbelief in her eyes, and yet he could also detect a faint glint of something else in her expression that was telling her that she could trust him.

"Ember, I know this all sounds insane, but..." he paused, wondering just how in the hell he was supposed to explain all of this to her, and not have her go bat-shit crazy. "Neoma's a witch," he went on finally, figuring that it might as well be all or nothing, "and she believes Evan was *befriended,* for lack of a better word, by this particular group of vampires because he has a unique psychic ability. It's extremely strong, and very rare. She thinks that he's always had the ability to read people's minds and to place suggestions into their thoughts without even knowing that he was doing it. She was trying to help him learn how to harness those abilities when Devlin and his family found out about it. He didn't just fall in with the wrong crowd, Ember, he was being *initiated* into it."

"*Vampires*?" She breathed, her voice no more than a whisper, and Bade nodded slowly. "You're talking about blood drinking, daylight hating *vampire's*?" She asked. "And, *not* the kind that sparkle in the sun or go to high school forever. Right?"

Bade nodded again, feeling like the biggest ass on the planet for having to be the one to dump all of this craziness on her, and implode her entire world in the middle of the night like this.

But, what choice did he have?

"And, this Devlin character," she croaked. "He *took* Evan? Just because he can read peoples' minds?"

"In part." Bade responded, dreading what was coming. "Contrary to popular belief, vampire's do not have the ability to control a victim's thoughts. *But,* if a person had those abilities *before* they were turned, those talents would magnify a hundred-fold. Once they became..." he hesitated, hating that he had to say the words, "the *undead*, they would be nearly unstoppable."

Ember's hand flew to her mouth and her eyes filled with tears as the reality of his words hit her like a sledgehammer. "You mean...they've turned him into one of them?" She gasped, and the pain he saw reflected in those amazing cinnamon depths cut him to the quick.

"Neoma doesn't believe so. At least not yet. In order to turn a human, that human must be a willing participant and drink from the leader of the family. It cannot be forced upon them."

"Oh, thank God."

"Ember," Bade went on, his heart aching for her. "Devlin and his family are cold, calculated, *vicious* killers. They won't hesitate in torturing your brother to bend him to their will and get what they want. And if they *are* coming after you now, it's because they need to use you as a bargaining chip to get Evan to submit to them. Your brother must be stronger than they had at first anticipated."

She nodded sadly, her gaze never wavering. "He always was a stubborn jackass," she told him as her mouth curved up ever so slightly at the corners, but there was just so much sadness there. "There was no changing his mind once it was made up. It used to drive me absolutely crazy when we were kids."

"Well, that just might be to our advantage," Bade replied, a glimmer of hope that there was still time welling up inside him. "But, we can't stay here. If Evan *was* sending you a message that you need to get away, we'd be wise to listen to him until I can track these assholes."

"Is that why you came here?" She asked suddenly. "Did you know that they found out about me and you were sent to keep an eye on me?"

"I was sent here to see if you could connect with Evan and help us find where they're keeping him," he replied honestly. "That's why Neoma gave you that coin. She knew that your wish would be to find your brother, and she knew it would open up the connection between the two of you. Which, obviously, it has if Evan is coming to you in your dreams."

She watched him for a very long moment, her brows furrowed together thoughtfully and he knew she was trying to take control of what had to be a million different thoughts and emotions swirling around in that pretty little head of hers.

"Ember," he said quietly, his eyes locking with and holding hers as he tried to convey to her that she could trust him to protect her. "I know this all seems pretty damned jacked-up, but you need to know that we are only trying to help you find your brother before it's too late."

After what seemed an eternity of heart-wrenching silence, she took a long, slow, steady breath of air and let it out with a resigned sigh.

"All right. What do we need to do?" She replied with a straightening of her spine. Her voice was laced with a stubborn conviction and strength that blew him away. "Will Neoma be all right if we leave?" She asked, her mouth tightening with worry.

"She's gone to her coven," he explained, his admiration of this woman growing by leaps and bounds with each minute that passed. "She'll be safest there."

She nodded; her lips set in a straight, stubborn line as her brow furrowed.

He admired that.

EMBER TOOK ANOTHER quick gulp of air into her lungs as she got her ragged emotions under control. This was just so twisted and messed up in so many ways that it was making her head spin, but she knew deep down in her gut that what this man was telling her was the absolute truth. She couldn't really explain *how* she knew it exactly. She just did. It was just a fact.

Now, she needed to figure out how in the hell to deal with it all and find Evan.

Holy Crap! She thought with a small little shake of her head.

Vampires? Witches? Really?

Ember pushed the thought away and stood up from the sofa. Bader had said that they needed to get out of here, and for all intents and purposes, so had Evan. So, if what they were conveying to her was true, they really needed to get their asses in gear.

"Where should we go?" She asked, and Bade stood up beside her.

"I have a cabin not too far from here. We'll hole up there while I try to track these bastards, and you work on your connection with your brother."

She felt her heart flutter around in her chest and tried to force it to settle.

Yes, her attraction to this man was undeniable, but it didn't mean a thing. He had been sent here to do a job. This wasn't going to be some romantic rendezvous. This wasn't a fun weekend getaway to wine country.

This wasn't anything but a man helping her to find her brother, and doing his best to keep her safe.

From freaking *Vampires!*

Good God.

"Let me just go change and pack a small bag," she said, trying hard to keep things as business-like as she possibly could, considering the fact that she was still sort of numb and the thought of spending time alone with him kept creeping into her thoughts. She turned and headed toward her bedroom. "I'll only be a minute."

She stopped suddenly as a thought occurred to her. She turned back and looked at him, struck by the intensity of his eyes as he met her gaze full on and she *knew* in that moment, and without a single doubt in her mind that she *could* trust this man standing there in front of her with her very life.

"Forgive me if I'm overstepping here, but I'm the curious type, and I really have to ask. Neoma's a witch. And, my *psychic* brother was taken by a group of vampires," she husked. "Just what in the hell are *you*? I mean...are you a witch too?"

"No," he responded simply, and she relaxed just a little bit more.

Thank God for small favors.

All this supernatural crap was beginning to make her head ache, and she really just needed a little bit of normalcy at the moment. That, and an aspirin the size of Texas.

"I'm a wolf shifter."

Her mouth dropped open for the second time in the last fifteen minutes as she tried to convince herself that she had to have heard him wrong.

But, she knew that she hadn't. If nothing else, she had always been blessed with exceptional hearing.

"You're a *werewolf?*" She rasped out, practically choking on the word.

Was he freaking kidding?

As if it wasn't bad enough that in the last few minutes she had been informed that her brother had been taken by a family of *vampires* for God's sake. Now, she was being told that she was being protected by freaking Lon Chaney, Jr.!

Holy Hell! What a cluster.

"Not exactly my first choice to describe it, but yes, I am," he replied with a knowing wink and a smug little grin, almost as if he could read her mind.

But, hell.

Who knew. Maybe he *could!*

Well. So much for normalcy.

CHAPTER FIVE

EMBER WAS STARTLED awake as the sound of gravel crunching under the tires of the SUV invaded her slumber. She pulled herself up a little straighter in the seat as she guiltily rubbed at her eyes with the backs of her hands.

She had dressed and hastily threw some things into a bag before she and Bader had hit the road, her body running on pure instinct.

They had only been driving for roughly about half an hour or so before she found herself fighting a valiant battle to stave off the overwhelming urge to drift off to sleep, and after they had stopped to grab some coffee and had gotten back in the car, her exhaustion had finally won out, and her eyes had drifted shut without her even realizing it.

"Oh, my God!" She apologized, her cheeks growing warm as a wave of embarrassment washed over her. "I didn't mean to fall asleep on you. You'd think with all the adrenaline rushing through me I would have been able to stay awake forever."

"The rush must have worn off, and you came crashing down," he replied with a chuckle. "It's perfectly fine. You needed the rest."

She watched out of the window as he made his way down a long, narrow drive framed by thick pines that smelled amazing. They pulled up to a beautiful, rustic cabin and she stared at it in wonder.

Complete with a wraparound porch and wooden swing, it was the type of place that just screamed *Home*.

"Wow," she murmured. "It's beautiful."

Bader pulled up in front and shut off the engine. "It's secluded, so you'll be safe here; but I do need you to know that my pack is not far away."

"Your *pack?*" She questioned, feeling her head beginning to reel once again.

He was actually part of a werewolf pack? Good gravy! This just kept getting weirder and weirder!

BADE OPENED HIS car door and slid from the seat. Trotting around, he pulled open hers and held out his hand to help her from the SUV.

When she hesitated, he gave her a reassuring grin. "Trust me, Sweetheart, it's safe. They'll leave us alone unless there's an emergency, and I'll have them patrol the area to make certain no one shows up without us knowing about it." When still she sat there staring at him with wide, uncertain eyes, he chuckled. "I solemnly swear that I won't bite," he promised, dragging his finger across his chest in the shape of an X. Right above where his heart thrummed against his ribcage. "Nor will any of my pack."

"Well, I certainly hope not," she huffed back at him, although her full, lush lips were curving up at the corners just the tiniest bit. He could still see the smallest hint of unease in her eyes, but she was fighting it well.

She finally let out a breath and took his hand, standing and stretching her feminine, lithe body as she did, and Bade's pulse began to race.

He cleared his throat and grabbed her bag from the trunk before resting his hand at the small of her back and directing her toward the house.

He unlocked the door, ushering her in ahead of him as the overwhelming feeling of...*rightness* hit him like a sucker punch to the throat. He watched in fascination as she made her way over the threshold and stopped in the entryway to survey the large open space, her eyes darting around with what he hoped to be pleasure.

Done in rich, warm reds and beautiful highly polished dark woods, this was the place he enjoyed being most in the world. It was his sanctuary. And, for the first time that he could recall, his cabin actually *did* feel like home.

"Wow," she breathed softly yet again as her eyes scanned the house.

"You like?"

She turned and met he gaze, her eyes sparkling with admiration. "Are you kidding me? I *love* it," she laughed with what could only be construed as awe lacing her words, and he felt himself swell with pride. For some reason, what she thought *mattered* to him. More than he we willing to admit.

"Follow me," he said, heading to the back of the cabin, and towards a long hallway. "I'll show you to your room and you can settle yourself in before I try to scrounge up something for us to eat."

She nodded silently as she followed close behind, and he tried to hide his grin when he heard her belly grumble at the mention of food.

EMBER WOKE FROM a deep sleep by the overpowering need to stop herself from screaming. It was harsh and brutal and it seized her in its grip like a vice.

She sat up with a shudder as she tried to remember what the dream had been about, but was coming up empty. All she knew was that she felt jittery and the dream was more of a nightmare with short flashes of places and people, and none of it was making her feel the least bit comforted.

The vision of glowing eyes and fangs skittered across her brain and she shivered again, even though the room seemed incredibly warm and stuffy.

She slipped from the bed and made her way over to the set of French doors on the far side of the bedroom which opened up to the back garden of Bader's cabin. She turned the lock and stepped through, hoping that the cool night air might help to clear her head a bit. Erase the tendrils of sleep that were clinging to her, so perhaps she could remember...*something* about her dream.

She glanced out at the thick woods surrounding the property, which were framed by a backdrop of snow-tipped mountains and smiled. It was amazing.

The moonlight kissed the area in a warm, silvery glow that was ethereal and tranquil, and she found herself feeling more relaxed here than she had in months. She didn't know what it was exactly, the crisp mountain air or something else, but it was a feeling she found herself enjoying more than she probably should.

"You really shouldn't be out here alone."

Ember spun around at the sound of the deep, masculine voice coming from the side of the cabin and watched in stunned silence as a tall, lanky blond walked around the corner and towards her.

A tall, lanky *naked* blond, she silently corrected herself as she adverted her eyes and met his gaze, doing her best to keep from bolting back inside like a frightened rabbit.

"Who are you?" She demanded with much more bravado than she would have thought considering that a very large part of her was terrified that the vampires had found them, and here she was, all alone and defenseless like a damned fool!

What in the hell had she been thinking coming out here alone?

She and Bader had spent the entire afternoon, and most of the evening talking and getting to know each other, and she realized now with a slight wince that she may have gotten a little too comfortable here.

And...it just might cost her dearly.

Shit!

"Damn it, Liam," Bader snapped from behind where Ember stood and she quickly spun back in the other direction to find him standing there so damn confidently, wearing only a loose pair of cotton shorts.

His magnificent chest bare, and sculpted and...

Oh, *Lord!*

"Sorry, boss," the man he had called Liam replied with an obviously amused little huff, and she turned back to find the blond surveying her body in a way that made her instantly uncomfortable, not to mention vulnerable considering the flimsy little nightshirt that she wore.

His appraisal of her was downright lecherous!

"I'm Liam," he informed her with a wicked grin as he stuck out his hand, which she took with hesitation.

"Ember Sloane. It's nice to meet you," she responded as politely as possible, but realized with a small wince that her reply was painfully stilted and clipped.

Bader stepped up behind her, the heat radiating off of his body warming her back in a way that was comforting, and she fought back the overpowering urge to sigh with relief.

The man just made her feel *safe*.

"Is there something that you need, Liam?" Bader asked, a puff of warm air hitting the back of her neck as he said the words.

She trembled.

Good God, but this man was dangerous!

"Not really," Liam replied with a chuckle, his eyes not leaving her for a moment. "I was just doing my rounds and spotted your *guest*. Figured I'd warn her about being outside alone." He gave her a wink that was anything but reassuring. "You just never know what lurks out there in the dark, and we can't be everywhere at once."

"Don't let us keep you then," Bader responded, his tone belying his obvious annoyance. "Please, just finish your sweep."

Liam gave him a quick nod.

"Will do," he chuckled, before turning and trotting off in the direction of the woods.

Ember watched in wonder as the man effortlessly *shifted* into a very large tan wolf. Not what she would have expected at all.

Holy shit!

Ember let out the breath she had been holding in a ragged rush as she watched the animal walk into the thick patch of trees and disappear from view.

Guess he really hadn't been kidding about being a werewolf and living with a pack!

Bader's strong, firm hand stationed itself on her hip and she fought back the overwhelming desire to lean back against that steely chest of his. She *knew* it would be amazing, but she just couldn't be that bold, so instead she forced the urge away.

"I know he's a bit...*crass,* and a complete asshole, but he's absolutely right about it not being safe out here alone," Bade whispered in her ear and the vision of his mouth descending on hers popped into her head like an exploding balloon and she fought to push it away with every ounce of willpower she had.

She really needed to keep her head in the game.

"I'm sorry," she apologized. She turned to look up at him and her breath caught in her throat as their eyes clashed.

He gazed back at her with a directness that was fierce and intense... and sexy as all hell.

"You were hot..." she replied only a moment before her face heated in mortification. "I...I mean...*I* was hot!" She exclaimed, wanting nothing more than to just melt right there through the ground at his feet. "It was stuffy and I was dreaming, and I woke up and couldn't fall back to sleep..."

Ember knew that she was blathering on, but she couldn't seem to stop herself. The way his mouth turned up at the corner as he silently watched her firmly insert her foot into her mouth, had her flustered as nothing ever had before!

So, she continued to prattle on and on...and on.

She silently begged her brain to wake-up and do its job! To stop the words that were pouring from her mouth like liquid stupid, but it didn't seem to be cooperating at the moment.

Gads! She *sucked*!

"I was trying to remember the dream and I needed air and...and..."

"Ember," he laughed, gently placing his finger against her lips and that simple gesture seemed to snap her traitorous brain out of whatever funk it had entered, and she clamped her mouth shut. "It's all right," he went on softly. "I just want to make sure that you're safe."

She nodded, not trusting herself to speak. Who knew what would come pouring out of her mouth next!

BADE WATCHED HER closely, painfully aware of the fact that his body was screaming at him to lean just forward and take those incredible lips. It was a deep, nagging need that was drilling into his gut and getting exceptionally difficult to resist.

Never being one to follow the rules, he did exactly what his body demanded of him and moved forward, taking her mouth with an urgency that was impossible to deny. There was no more debating or fighting it. It was what he *needed* to do. His arms wrapped around her tiny frame and he pulled her close as his mouth devoured hers.

He was more than just pleasantly surprised when he realized that her delicate fingers were sliding up his arms and curling themselves in his hair, holding fast and tugging him closer.

He broke the contact and leaned back just enough to look into her eyes, not wanting to give up even the slightest bit of space between their bodies. The feeling of her smooth, curved frame against his hard one was sublime.

THE WOLF NEXT DOOR

The raw desire that he saw reflected in her expression no doubt mirrored his own and he groaned from the very recesses of his chest, as if in agony.

He knew in that moment that there was *definitely* going to be no turning back now.

Even if he had wanted to. Which he did not.

His hands lifted and framed her perfect face as he watched the desire snap and crackle in her eyes.

He was in awe.

"Ember," he husked out, not quite certain what it was that he wanted to say. He just needed her to know that he wanted her. More in that moment in time than he had ever wanted anything else before.

She looked up at him, a playful grin curving her mouth, and shook her head before pulling his back down to hers and nibbling at his lower lip only a moment before taking his mouth once again in silent invitation.

He felt a ripple of adrenaline race up his spine as he returned her embrace for all he was worth, sweeping her up into his arms and carrying her back through the open French Doors.

Bade took his sweet time as he slid her down his body, his hands moving across her to grab the hem of her nightshirt and pull it up and over her head, breaking their kiss for only the second that it took to remove it. Her mouth was the sweetest nectar he had ever tasted, and he was a thirsty man.

He could feel her breasts pressing against his chest, her hardened peaks begging for his attention.

He had no choice but to oblige.

He moved his mouth slowly down her neck to the dip of her collarbone, and over her heated flesh. He greedily took her nipple into his mouth, his tongue tasting and teasing and pulling a sexy as hell sound from the recesses of her belly that caused him to shiver. His skin was alive and rippling with desire.

And, his wolf howled.

EMBER WAS RIDING a wave of pure, unadulterated lust, and didn't care a single whit if the world exploded around them at that particular moment in time.

When this amazing man's hot, *oh so skilled,* mouth made contact with her nipple, she was pretty sure she had died and was floating around some kind of amazing astral plain of unbelievable pleasure.

And she was fine with that.

The feel of his hands on her body, and his mouth at her breast was like nothing she had ever experienced before in her entire life.

It was primal. It was demanding. It was fan-freaking-tastic!

"Bader," she husked, her voice nothing more than a strangled whisper. "*Please.*"

She wasn't quite sure what she was asking of him. She just simply knew that she *would* die without it.

He lifted his face and gave her a grin that nearly stopped her heart in her chest before lifting her up, only to drop her back down onto the mattress.

A giggle erupted from her as she bounced against the bed. She stared up at him, her tongue darting out to lick her lips as watched in fascination as he slid out of the shorts he wore. His magnificent form the stuff Gods were made of.

The proof of his desire sprang forward as he hastily dropped them to the floor and she shuddered with anticipation.

And once again, for the second time that night, all she could think was...*Holy Shit!*

He reached over and pulled the silk underwear she wore down her legs and tossed them behind him, his eyes almost glowing now with a heat that was undeniable and erotic.

Ember's eyes traveled over his body without the slightest hesitation or shyness. There was none of that. There was only a deep yearning.

He slid down onto the bed beside her and pulled her against him, his mouth taking hers again with promise as he slid his hand down her leg and pulled it up over his waist.

"Christ, Sweetheart, I want you so bad I ache," he growled against her mouth, his voice low and fierce as their breath mingled, and she couldn't help but smile.

Now *that* was the understatement of the century!

"You have me," she murmured in reply and felt his chest vibrate against hers with the groan that rumbled from him.

He kissed her quickly before turning his attention to more pressing matters. He began moving down her body at a leisurely pace. His teeth nipped and his tongue soothed as he made his way torturously over her skin. Leaving, in his wake, a trail of sublime sensation that she was sure would set her body ablaze.

Her skin tingled with an incredible low hum wherever he happened to touch, or kiss...or nibble and she bit down on her bottom lip to keep from screaming to the point that she tasted blood.

When his hot, skilled mouth *finally* met the apex of her thighs, she curled her toes into the mattress as she grabbed the sheets and twisted, trying her with everything she had not to lose her sanity.

His fingers almost intuitively ghosted across her body before moving to where his mouth was painstakingly working its magic, and slipped inside.

Her orgasm was almost immediate, and she cried out his name on a gasp as she went catapulting through the stratosphere. Stars exploded and danced behind her tightly closed eyes as she frantically gulped for air. Her breath slipping between her lips in quick ragged puffs, and she swore that her eyes were going to be permanently rolled back in her head after that!

She was vaguely aware of the feel of his body as he slid his way back up, torturously slow, and his mouth placed soft, gentle kisses at the curve of her neck.

His weight against her was curiously comforting, yet erotic as all hell, and she found herself wiggling slightly to let him know that she was waiting for him.

In fact, it was as if she needed this man more than she needed the air she was so greedily breathing in at the moment.

Bader pulled her earlobe between his teeth and gave it a gentle tug as he moved his body just enough to join them, and she sighed.

She grazed his chin with her teeth and he caught her gaze, his intense eyes alight with a passion that was honest and almost primal and her heart skipped a beat.

BADE BEGAN TO move his body, slowly at first, just to allow himself a moment to revel in the indescribable sensation of being buried deep inside of this woman. It was surreal. It was awe-inspiring!

It was…*Shit!*

Bade stopped as the realization hit him square in the chest with all the gentleness of a nuclear explosion.

This woman was his mate!

Holy freaking *crap*! This was not *at all* what he had been expecting!

The enormity of it all crashed down on him like a ton of bricks, and he tried to get his thoughts together. He had to think! But, when only a moment later, his *mate* kissed her way up his neck in order to seek out his mouth, all rational thought flew straight out of the damned window.

He moved his body, his strides strong and steady and she met his pace to absolute perfection. But, why wouldn't she?

She was his God-damned mate!

Just what in the hell was he going to do now?

He didn't do feelings! He didn't do forever! He sure as hell didn't do domestic bliss!

He increased his movements as he sensed her climbing to that place where she was reaching her pinnacle yet again, and did his best to hold back so he could hit that precipice with her.

Finally, he felt her begin to climax, her body tightening around him as his name passed her lips in a throaty cry and he let himself go, stunned by the impact of his release. His entire body vibrated from it like it never had before, and he found himself thinking that domestic bliss didn't sound half bad. Not if she was the one that he was going to share it with.

Shit and hellfire. He was completely screwed!

A smile curved his mouth as the thought popped into his head that he really couldn't say that he minded much at all.

Let him burn.

Bade slid beside her and pulled her into the crook of his arm. Christ, but he found himself loving the feel of her soft, pliable, *amazing* body fitted snugly up against his, and he kissed the top of her head as her warm breath tickled his chest.

Yep. He was screwed.

EMBER CURVED HER body against this man's incredible frame and fought for all she was worth to keep her eyes from sliding shut. She was satiated, and content, and sleepy.

He made her feel safe and protected, and she just wanted to fall asleep in his arms and sleep a long, dreamless slumber. A slumber safe from the terrors that waited in the fog. Secure in the fact that he was with her, and would let nothing harm her.

As if reading her thoughts, she felt his lips brush against her temple before whispering *"Rest,"* into her ear.

She obliged.

She was just *that* secure.

CHAPTER SIX

"EMBER..."

Embers eyes fluttered opened and she glanced across the darkened bedroom, trying to get her bearings. She could hear Bader snoring lightly against her ear as her head rested on his enormous chest and a small smile curved her lips.

Was she *really* lying here in this man's arms?

A part of her wanted to pinch herself, just to make sure she wasn't dreaming, but there was that other part of her who was so afraid that if she did, she would indeed wake up from this bliss.

She nibbled at her bottom lip as she found herself wondering what had woken her. Nothing seemed off. In fact, everything was near perfection.

She laid there quietly a moment longer, listening to the sound of Bader's even breathing as it cut through the silence of the bedroom, and allowed herself just a bit more time to enjoy the pleasure of being wrapped in his embrace.

It was surreal.

She indulged herself only a few precious moments more before reluctantly slipping away from his perfect frame and carefully sliding from the bed; taking extra care not to wake him.

She must have been dreaming of Evan again, she surmised as she snagged Bader's t-shirt from the floor and silently headed toward the kitchen to grab a glass of water. She was absolutely parched, and just wanted to grab something, then crawl back into bed to snuggle up with the sleeping Adonis lying there.

Who knew how long she would have to enjoy this feeling? The man would certainly come to his senses sooner, rather than later.

"*Ember.*"

She jumped as the sound of her name drifted across the air. Floating on the breeze like a feather in a wind.

It *was* Evan! She *knew* it to the very marrow of her bones.

And, it was coming from right outside!

Without thinking, she hurriedly made her way through the kitchen and to the back door of the house, moving purely on instinct now as the thought of seeing her brother again hit her full force.

She reached out and pulled open the door, her eyes scanning the area in search of any sign of him, and bit back a squeal of delight when she spotted her twin standing across the yard, the excitement hitting her and sending her senses reeling.

She *hadn't* been dreaming!

She took a few steps forward and towards where he stood, but stopped, hesitating as her eyes adjusted to the darkness and his features became clearer. He was deathly pale. His skin almost translucent in the moonlight, and he was so thin, and bedraggled. She watched in stunned silence as his body swayed slightly from side to side as he seemed to struggle to stay erect.

He merely stood there…silent, his face devoid of any emotion whatsoever as he stared straight ahead, almost as if in a trance, and it unnerved her to her core.

Something wasn't right.

In the blink of an eye, Evan was flanked by several men, dressed all in black; their lifeless, silvery eyes glowing in the darkness like an animals reflecting the beams of light from a passing car, and the sight of them appearing around her brother without any warning caused a shudder to run across her.

They were absolutely terrifying. Like nothing she had ever seen before.

Ember took a long, shaky breath as she tried to calm her nerves and the overwhelming urge to turn and run swept over her as she was hit with a sense of impending doom.

It descended over her like a thick, black cloud, practically suffocating her with its noxious presence.

This was so not good at all.

BADE'S EYES FLEW open as his entire body snapped to attention with all the subtlety of being hit by a train. His senses screamed out to him that something was dangerously amiss.

He found Ember's space next to him empty and cool to the touch, and jumped from the bed as if he had been set on fire, his eyes searching the room for any sign of her, only to find everything deathly still.

To still.

He could feel the air around him crackling with that all too familiar electrical current of danger and quickly slipped into his jeans and left the room.

Something was very, *very* wrong.

"EVAN," EMBER BREATHED out, as she unconsciously took another step toward her brother, glaring in fury at the creatures standing so stoically beside him, their mouths twisted up into something loosely resembling sneers as they watched her intently with an almost humor-filled curiosity.

That...and a look of what could only be described as...*hunger.* It was almost as if she were the fly, and they the spiders.

"Your sister is truly lovely," the man standing directly to Evans left exclaimed as his glittering, cold eyes surveyed her from head to toe. Her skin began to crawl as her stomach roiled. His blatant perusal of her left her feeling violated and dirty, and she wanted nothing more than to scratch the bastard's eyes out.

The timber of his voice was strong and commanding...almost *feral,* and Ember found herself despising him immediately. The arrogance radiated off of him in waves, like a stench that grabbed hold and wouldn't let go, and she knew without a doubt that this *douchebag* had to be the leader of this little band of assholes.

Her temper simmered as she stared back at the group, refusing to cower.

"Give me my brother," she ground out, not sure just what in the hell she thought she was going to do if they refused her demand, but she'd be damned if she was going to just stand here and do *nothing.*

"My, my...she *is* a feisty little thing, isn't she?" he chortled in response with an amused little huff. "It really is such a shame that we must to kill her. A waste, really, but she is a means to an end." He turned toward Evan and gave him a quick shove, propelling her brother forward on legs that trembled violently. "Time to say your goodbyes."

Evan stumbled, nearly falling to his knees, which caused Ember to rush towards him.

"No!"

The sound of her twin's voice blasted through her brain with such force that she actually saw stars. She stopped dead in her tracks, staring back at him with her mouth hanging open in shock when she realized that his lips hadn't moved to shout the word at her.

He was in her head! Bader had been right! This really *was* why the vampires wanted him so badly!

"Don't let them get too close, Emmie," Evan warned, and she found herself taking a step back at his command.

Before she had even a millisecond to gather her thoughts and decide what to do, one of the creatures came rushing at her at an inhuman speed and had her by the throat.

He pulled her over to where their leader stood as she struggled and fought to break free, but she was no match for the strength of these men.

"Easy, Yuri," the leader warned the vampire holding onto her in a grip that was completely cutting off her supply of air and causing her eyes to water. "We mustn't dispose of her just yet." He looked to Evan who had finally succumbed to his weakness and was now down on his hands and knees, bracing himself up on arms that shook frantically. "I haven't yet gotten what I desire."

"And just what would that be, Devlin? A stake through that miserable black thing of yours that poses for a heart?"

The sound of Bader's voice washed over Ember like a tidal wave of warmth, and her heart skipped a beat.

"YOU'RE LOOKING WELL, Bade." Devlin chuckled with a snide little grin, and Bade felt his entire body tense as his wolf howled in fury.

He had run into Devlin LaPorte on more than one occasion in his days as a hunter, and the bastard had always managed to give him the slip somehow.

Well...he'd be damned if he'd let him get away this time!

"Let her go," he demanded icily of the vampire holding onto Ember in a death grip.

"You seem to be outnumbered, Bade," Devlin laughed.

"Really?" Bade responded, his voice low and even as his lip curled up in a sneer. Several very large wolves stepped out from the darkness of the surrounding woods.

His pack had arrived as he knew they would.

He watched with amusement as the four Vampire's looked around in surprise, carefully weighing their options and looking to their leader for direction.

DEVLIN GRABBED EMBER from Yuri and wrapped her in his arms, his lips pulling back as his fangs descended from his gums. He yanked her head to the side, revealing the alabaster skin of her neck, where her pulse fluttered sporadically with her terror.

She smelled positively delicious, and he found his bloodlust rising.

"It's all very simple, really. They attack…" He informed him coolly, nodding at the wolves. "I drink. Do you really think that you will be fast enough to save her before I've drained her dry? Are you feeling *that* lucky, Bade?"

He knew that the wolf leader was ready to explode with his rage, and was counting on just that. His obvious regards for the tiny human held so snugly in his embrace would hopefully be his nemesis's downfall.

Emotions and feelings were very rarely ever a good thing. They served no purpose whatsoever.

EMBER'S GAZE COLLIDED with Bade's and held fast, as she tried her best to convey to him all that he had come to mean to her in such a short amount of time. She needed him to know that he mattered to her. No matter what happened, she wanted him to know that she cared.

"Kill them," she croaked out finally in defiance, only a millisecond before all hell broke loose.

Evan, who it seemed as if everyone had forgotten about for the moment, suddenly pushed himself back up to his feet as his voice exploded in her head once again.

Duck!

Ember instinctively let herself go limp and slid down Devlin's body just far enough that Evan had room to hit the vampire square in the face with a solid crack to his large, pointy nose.

The vampire's hold on her loosened, more from surprise she was guessing, than the actual punch, and she dropped the rest of the way down to the ground, kicking out and hitting the bloodsucker in the shin with everything that she had in her. Praying that she could at least stall him long enough so that the pack could make their move.

She stared in absolute wonder and awe as Bader shifted into a striking jet-black wolf.

Strong, powerful...he was magnificent!

And huge!

Growls and screeches boomed around them as the wolves took her cue and used that precise moment of distraction to attack, and she watched the unfolding battle in stunned fascination as Bader sprang through the air and slammed into Devlin with a mighty smack, his muscular body knocking the vampire to the ground in one fail swoop. He began snapping furiously at the vampire's throat as the bloodsucker shrieked in fury.

She stared as the two of them sparred, unable to move, almost as if she were frozen to the spot until she realized someone was pulling on her arm and turned to see Evan on his hands and knees beside her, that mischievous smile she knew all too well cutting across his features.

He was frighteningly pale and his breathing was labored, and she knew that it had taken what little strength he had left to knock that asshole in the face as he had, but her brother was *there*. Those sons of bitches hadn't broken him! She could see it in his eyes.

He was still there.

"Come on, Em, you need to *move!*" he urged her, trying to push himself unsteadily to his feet, and as if she had been slapped, she sprang into action.

She stood and wrapped her arm around his waist, pulling him up and leading him over towards a small stone retaining wall at the back of the garden. She eased him down onto it and hugged him fiercely only a moment before turning to watch the melee happening around them and trying to figure out what she could do to could help.

Bader and Devlin rolled and slammed against the ground, fangs snapping and punches flying as each grappled to regain dominance. Finally, with a mighty roar Bader hit his mark and the vampire screamed in agony before falling still.

The other vampires who were left, made a horrible hissing sound in what could only be construed as fright, and took off running, the fight leaving them the instant that their leader perished.

The wolves followed close at their heels, and she knew that they didn't stand a chance.

Ember looked back toward Bader who had shifted back and was standing there in all his striking glory. Their gazes locked as he gave her that heart stopping grin that made her weak in the knees and before she knew what was happening, she realized that she was running toward him.

He welcomed her into his embrace as his head dipped and his lips met hers. He kissed her soundly, *thoroughly,* and she soared through the stratosphere with just his touch.

Talk about an adrenaline rush!

Holy crap!

He broke away much too soon, and looked into her eyes a moment before his gaze slipped down to her neck and his expression changed to one of anger. She was pretty sure that she had bruises there, and she cupped the side of his face in her hand in a gesture to reassure him the only way she could.

"Are you, all right?" He asked softly and she nodded, her throat constricting with emotion at his obvious concern for her.

"You were amazing," she husked in awe.

"You weren't too bad yourself," he chuckled in reply. "Are you sure that you're okay?"

She giggled lightly as her eyes gleamed. "Well, my lips are a bit sore," she informed him, her brow lifting suggestively.

Bader leaned forward and brushed his mouth against hers. "Are they, now?" He asked with a wicked chuckled that reverberated through his chest and into hers. "I just might have to remedy that situation."

"I believe you might," she responded softly.

With that he kissed her again and she shivered straight down to the tips of her toes.

Oh, hell and *shitfire*...she was falling hard for this man!

"Um, I really hate to interrupt this tender moment and all, but if you're going to insist on sucking face with my sister, I'd really prefer to not have to watch it. Especially considering that you're buck naked!" Evan called from where he sat, and Ember smiled. "Besides, I'm starving! Those bastards didn't believe in common hospitality."

Bade glanced her brother's way and gave him a grin. "Nice to see you again, Evan," he laughed before taking her lips once more.

EPILOGUE

EMBER ONCE AGAIN stood by the fountain, a small, content sigh whispering past her lips as she stared down into the rippling water. It seemed a lifetime ago that she had stood in this exact spot, making a wish that she never would have ever thought would come true.

And now…

Strong, familiar arms wrapped themselves around her from behind and she was pulled back against that solid, muscular frame she knew by touch. That scent that she loved tickling her nose as it drifted on the air.

Bade nuzzled her neck as his hands fanned out over her burgeoning belly.

"Where it all began," he murmured against her ear.

"Who would have thought?" She replied with a smile, reflecting on how very much her life had changed over the past six months.

They had brought Evan back home where Neoma had immediately burst into tears before hovering over him like a mother hen and doing everything short of force feeding him in order to bring him back to full-strength.

She and Bade had stayed around long enough to make certain the vampires had given up their pursuit of Evan now that their ringleader and most of his *family* had been permanently disposed of.

They spent time enjoying getting to know each other, and when Bade had proposed to her after they stood up for Evan and Neoma as they exchanged vows, she had happily accepted.

This man was her soul-mate. Of that she had absolutely no doubt. He was her destiny. Her future.

Her *everything*.

One month later, they married. Two months after that...they discovered they were pregnant.

Now, they were ready to go back to Bade's cabin and ready themselves to welcome their new addition.

"*Our cabin,*" he gently corrected her and she huffed with feigned irritation.

"I'm not sure I'll ever get used to you being able to read my thoughts. It's creepy," she scolded him. "It's bad enough my brother can get inside my head. Now I have to worry about you too!"

"That's what you get for agreeing to bond with a Wolf shifter," he responded with a playful nip to her earlobe. "But, no worries, my love. You'll be reading my thoughts in no time. It just takes a bit longer for you *humans*."

Ember leaned her head back against the curve of his shoulder and smiled. "I'm not sure I *want* to know what's going on in there," she teased.

"I'm pretty sure you can guess," Bade retorted as he ground himself against her backside. "Come on, use Neoma's gift and let's head home. I'm anxious to have you all to myself for a while."

Ember looked down at the coin held tightly in her hand.

So much like the first one Neoma had given her.

The only difference between the two was this one had the intricate stamp of vines intertwining around a heart instead of a dragon's head.

Neoma had insisted she take it, telling her that she had been kind enough to use her wish to give Neoma her heart back by bringing Evan home, Ember deserved a wish strictly for herself.

Ember set the coin down on the edge of the fountain before turning and wrapping her arms around her mate's neck.

"Let's leave the coin for someone else," she husked against his mouth. "I've got everything I could ever wish for."

ABOUT THE AUTHOR

DARLENE KUNCYTES WAS born and raised in Northeast Ohio and still happily resides there with her spoiled rotten fur-babies. She has loved losing herself to reading and writing for as long as she can remember and has always had a special place in her heart for romance. She's got a wicked sense of humor who loves to find the humor in everyday life and believes that anything is absolutely possible as long as you believe it is! And, yes…she is exceedingly, and sometimes disgustingly happy! Life is way too short to waste a moment of it hating!

She is currently hard at work on the fourth novel in The Supernatural Desire Series – Harper's Heavenly Embrace!

You can find all of Darlene's books on Amazon and at Barnes and Noble.

For more information on Darlene, visit her at:

WWW.DARLENEKUNCYTES.COM

Printed in Great Britain
by Amazon

67107883R00051